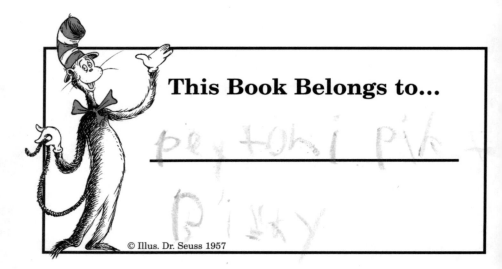

This Book Belongs to...

peytoni pik

Pixxy

© Illus. Dr. Seuss 1957

MARC BROWN

ARTHUR'S READING RACE

BEGINNER BOOKS
A division of Random House, Inc.

Text and illustrations copyright © 1996 by Marc Brown.
All rights reserved under International and Pan-American Copyright Conventions.
Published in the United States by Random House, Inc., New York, and
simultaneously in Canada by Random House of Canada Limited, Toronto. Originally
published by Random House, Inc., in 1996 as a Step into Reading® book.

Library of Congress Cataloging-in-Publication Data:
Brown, Marc Tolon. Arthur's reading race / written and illustrated by Marc Brown.
p. cm. SUMMARY: Arthur doesn't believe that his little sister can really read, so he
challenges her to prove it. ISBN 0-679-86738-4 (pbk.: alk. paper). — ISBN 0-679-
96738-9 (lib. bdg.: alk. paper).
[1. Reading—Fiction. 2. Brothers and sisters—Fiction. 3. Aardvark—Fiction.] I.
Title. PZ7.B81618Arq 1995 [E]—dc20 95-38987

Printed in the United States of America
10 9 8 7 6 5 4 3 2 1

Arthur learned to read
in school.

Now Arthur reads everywhere!
He reads in the car.

He reads in bed.

He reads
to his puppy, Pal.

Arthur even reads
to his little sister, D.W.

One day Arthur said,
"I can teach YOU to read, too."
"I already know how to read,"
said D.W.

"You do not!" said Arthur.
"Do too!" said D.W.

"Prove it," said Arthur.
"Read ten words, D.W.,
    and I'll buy you an ice cream."

D.W. stuck out her hand.
"It's a deal," she said.
"Let's go!"

They raced to the park.

Arthur pointed to a sign.

"What's that say?" he asked.

"Zoo," said D.W.

"Easy as pie."

"I spy three words," said Arthur.

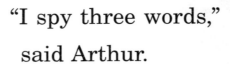

"Me too," said D.W.

"Taxi, gas, milk."

Arthur stepped off the curb.

"Look out!" said D.W.

"It says Don't Walk.

You could get hit by a car."

"All right,
Miss Smarty-Pants,
what's that say?"
asked Arthur.

"Police," said D.W.
"And you better
keep off the grass
or the police will get you."

"Bank," said D.W.

"I have a bank.

I hide my money in it

so you can't find it.

Bank makes eight words."

"We're almost home,"
said Arthur.
"Too bad.
You only read eight words.
No ice cream
for you today."

"Hold your horses," said D.W.

"I spy...ice cream.

Hot dog! I read ten words.

Let's eat!"

pizza chip   shoe lace

Bumpy road   moose ripple

frog chip

egg shell

D.W. and Arthur ran

to the ice cream store.

Arthur bought two big cones.

Strawberry for D.W.
and chocolate for himself.
"Yummy," said D.W.

Arthur sat down.

"Sit down with me," said Arthur,

"and I'll read you my book."

"No," said D.W.

"I'll read YOU the book."

Arthur shook his head.

"I don't think so," he said.

"There are too many words
that you don't know."

D.W. laughed.

"Get up, Arthur."

"Now I can teach you
two words that you don't know,"
said D.W.
"WET PAINT!"